A Trick of Light

A Collection of Four Supernatural Short Stories

Cora Zane

Grrl X Publishing

Author's Notes: *The Ghost Train* originally appeared as a featured story on the Midnight Moon Café paranormal blog, which is now defunct. The story was later reprinted in *Weirdly 2*, an anthology published by Wild Child Publishing. *A Trick of Light* originally appeared in *Weirdly 2*, published by Wild Child Publishing. Prince of Thorns originally appeared in Ultimate Angels: Tales of Winged Warriors, published by KnightWatch Press, an imprint of Fringeworks.

Table of Contents

The Ghost Train

The letter came from my grandmother's attic. I found it, along with a string of other old mementos, in a dusty straw purse at the bottom of an antique armoire. I'd been clearing out Nana's things for a few weeks, ever since my brothers insisted we finally sell the farm.

While it pained me to see this chunk of property end up outside of the family circle, I had to agree the house was located too far away from the rest of us, and no one had the time or money for the upkeep. Selling was the only way to ensure the place would receive the proper routine maintenance an older home requires.

As it happened, once we'd all agreed to sell, the sad task of sorting Nana's things fell to me. Among the remnants of her long life, the purse I uncovered in the armoire seemed at first like another one of those treasures too personal to throw out.

Embroidered with purple and mauve thistles and other decorative fronds sewn right onto the weave, the bag had no closure, only two round cane handles that when held together closed the purse. Pretty, but dated.

My grandmother had always liked things like that, items that had been in style during her heyday, which was somewhere around the time of the Second World War. By the looks of it, this bag had been very well loved. I pulled it from the drawer, my heart aching. I shook my head. How I missed her.

I was disappointed to discover on closer inspection that the bag was flat as an old shoe and crushed toward the bottom.

I decided it wasn't worth salvaging after all. That stung a little because something about the purse drew me—I couldn't have guessed what, since I certainly had no use for a straw bag.

Nevertheless, I checked inside for anything important and found an embroidered hair ribbon, a powder compact with a cracked mirror, a packet of tissues, and an old letter, which was resting on its side and pressed flat against the inner lining of the bag.

I tossed the other things into the trash bin and turned my attention to the letter, which was folded four square, the paper amber with age. It had crumpled from moisture like the dried petals of a pressed flower, and I opened it very carefully so the corner folds wouldn't tear.

I don't know what I expected exactly. It was preserved so well, I assumed it must be an old love letter from Howard, my grandfather. He'd been a man of few words, although at some point he'd bragged to us grandkids about the wooing of his lovely Rosalie. I'd been about ten or so when he'd told us the story of how he'd stolen our nana from another man, a soldier who, at the time, had been stationed in Hawaii, or some other far-flung place.

I thought about that story now and decided whatever this letter turned out to be, it was obviously something special for Nana to have kept it all these years. After Grandpa died, I'd asked her if she'd saved any personal letters he'd written to her when they were 'courting'. I wanted to add them to the family archive I'd been building for the last thirty years or so. However, it seemed I was out of luck. She told me if there had ever been any letters, she definitely didn't have them now. She'd never been much of a "pen and paper gal", she'd explained. A good thing, I suppose, since Grandpa apparently never had much inclination to express, in written form at least, any poetic feelings he might've had for her.

So this new find was a curiosity. I looked at the letter as an unusual artifact to add to the family scrapbook. The rarity of it excited me, even though it saddened me a little to imagine my grandparents young and in love. After all, that was another life, and Nana had not been gone from us for very long. Grief still nagged me at the slightest provocation.

I smoothed the letter flat against my thigh, glad to see that the ink remained fair. The body of the text was still legible. The words had only bled a tiny bit. I lifted the page to see it better in the window light and read the first few words. An odd chill came over me.

Dearest Rosalie,

I know all about him. I wish I didn't, but I can't change what is. I love you even now, and despite what your mother says, there is still time for you to change your mind. I will be arriving at Kilkirkin Station at 7:15 p.m.

If you love me still, meet me there. Even if you cannot bring yourself to come away with me in the end, at the very least, I would have you stand face to face with me and tell me goodbye. I will be waiting.

Love always.

The letter was unsigned.

My throat constricted. I let the top of the letter fold down. I never knew my grandmother had a lover, and the discovery of it shocked me. Neither had I suspected that the soldier Grandpa had mentioned all those years ago had been anyone serious, or that he had truly made a move toward my grandmother beyond the terms of possibly a light flirtation. Nana had been old fashioned right to the very end, as faithful as a temple priest. She had certainly never mentioned a love interest in anyone other than my grandfather, to whom she'd been married for close to fifty years.

I will be waiting.

Had he come? Had he waited? Did Nana meet him to tell him goodbye? Did my grandfather know anything at all about this? Somehow I doubted it.

My grandfather's stories of wooing struck home, and I felt sorry for the young man who'd written this letter. Obviously, Nana had stayed with Grandpa. However, that didn't stop the sudden surge of questions from flowing through my mind, questions that would never have any conclusive answers because whatever secrets my grandmother might've had, she'd carried them with her to her grave.

This played on my mind for the rest of the day. Between pulling out boxes and sorting furniture, off and on I stopped to reread that letter. As much as I loved my grandparents, sadness for this unknown man gripped me.

For hours I sifted through layer upon layer of tangible memories, old clothes and knick-knacks, and any number of odd trinkets forgotten in that dusty attic, until at last the light of the day faded to dusk. The electricity had been turned off shortly after Nana's death, and I wasn't about to bother fighting with the old generator. Before it got too dark to see my way around the house, I gathered my purse and my keys and locked up for the night.

While driving the twenty miles back to Powkeaton where I had rented a hotel room for the weekend, it occurred to me that I'd be driving right past the old Kilkirkin depot.

The rail line there had died out long ago, the tracks left abandoned as modern roads cut new paths through the Northern Plains and other modes of long distance transportation became more feasible for the average person. At one time, it had been a bustling station, a major layover point for travelers heading out west. Its former glory now sat reduced to the likeness of a crumbling barn.

The station came into view and something possessed me to pull over. Knowing what I knew now, I felt it was only right that I stop by the depot to stand in for my grandmother, who couldn't be there to say goodbye.

Of course, this grand idea would have to come to me at night. I sat for a minute on the shoulder of the road, thinking hard before finally getting out. The moon passed in and out of the thick cloud cover. My only source of light came from the headlights of the rental car.

The old station resembled a black, sagging box in the darkness. The stillness of it spooked me. The useless train tracks stretched away from the depot, cutting into the weed-choked ground like a scar on the face of the land. The silhouette of sorrel grass waved in the night breeze, and in the overgrown field several yards out from the depot, there was a squat, weed-choked building with a caved in roof. When I'd passed by the depot earlier in the day, I'd noticed a rusted boxcar parked beneath the rubble, but it was lost in the shadows now.

I didn't get too close to the depot, but I did walk a reasonable distance from the car. The rutted earth was difficult to walk across, even with the headlights pointed at it. Once or twice, I tripped on clumps of dried grass that appeared to be little more than shadows on the ground ahead of me. It was a wonder I didn't twist an ankle.

When my elongated shadow finally blended into the surrounding darkness, I stopped and faced the barn-like structure beside the tracks. It looked on the verge of collapse. Standing in the open air of the plains, I felt at once free and yet incredibly vulnerable. The summer wind tugging at my hair smelled of dust and the coming rain. To calm my nerves, I inhaled deeply.

Now that I was here, I glanced around not exactly sure what to do. I was just about to turn and leave when, out of nowhere, a whistle shrieked. Panic shot through me.

An old-fashioned train with a single stack appeared in the distance. It thundered along the tracks, and my jaw dropped in stunned disbelief.

The old locomotive belched thick white smoke that billowed around the body of the train like a pale mist. Goose bumps chased up and down my arms as I focused on the single headlight cutting through the darkness.

I wanted to run, but fear held me rooted to the spot. The sound of the approaching train was so loud it vibrated in the hollows of my bones. It shook the ground, the frightening power of it somehow able to reach me through the open air. Would the train stop at the station? The idea horrified me and intrigued me at the same time.

Heart hammering, I hurried to a better vantage point to watch the train pass the deserted station.

By the time I reached the rental car, the train was rushing by. The sound was deafening, but odd. It was muffled the way a ticking clock is softened when smothered by a pillow. I watched the train pass behind the crumbling depot, and then I glanced to my left, where the tracks led away from the station and into the plains. The train never emerged from the other end.

The sound faded, and then vanished as though it had never been. No signs of smoke lingered in the air. No distant glare of a headlight cut through the surrounding fields.

Perhaps the train had stopped at Kilkirkin Station after all.

Shaking all over, I climbed back into the rental car and shut the door. I sat there trying to regain my nerves, and that's when I noticed the green glow of the digital clock on the dashboard. It read *7:17.*

My blood ran cold.

Never in a million years could I have explained exactly what I'd just witnessed. In truth, I still can't quite wrap my mind around it. That night, numb from shock, I pulled back onto the road and drove onward to Powkeaton as though nothing had happened.

Had the train been real? Could it have been a private engine traveling by permission on the abandoned line, or was it just a figment of my imagination? Maybe the train had been carrying the ghost of my grandmother's lover, still hoping to find his beloved Rosalie waiting there after all this time. Perhaps Nana's ghost had been there waiting just as I had done, hoping to take care of unfinished business.

There's no way I can ever know for sure.

The house has sold since then, so I have no reason to go back. My only hope is that whatever spirits stopped by the Kilkirkin train station that night, they have since moved on to their eternal rest.

A Trick of Light

"*Goodbye* Mississippi."

I glance over at Clarice. It's the first thing she's said in at least fifty miles, and the look on her face tells me she means absolute business about getting home as soon as possible.

Her brown eyes glitter in the darkness, and her mouth curves into a thin line while she concentrates on driving. Every few minutes she glances into the rearview mirror at the cars behind us. Each time, the reflection of white headlights strikes the mirror at just the right angle so a huge rectangular glare cuts a swatch across her face.

Although I'm eager to be home, the steady beat of the windshield wipers has made me drowsy. The pattering rain plays a steady, white noise symphony, a soothing lullaby, in the relative silence of my sister's car. I have no problem with the traffic or Clarice's defensive driving as long as she gets me to my destination sooner rather than later.

Tired and groggy, I gave up driving two rest stops back, and once I see that the Saturday night traffic in Vicksburg is heavy despite the weather, I'm glad I'm no longer behind the wheel. The closer we get to the final exits facing the Mississippi River Bridge, the thicker the traffic seems to get.

Clarice swears under her breath and taps the brake, and I tear my gaze from her profile to look at the road ahead. I sit a little straighter and grip the armrest, dazzled by the flood of red taillights glowing in a steady stream along the right lane of the interstate.

The nearest off-ramp is clogged with bumper-to-bumper traffic. The final exit leading around to all the riverfront hotels and casinos is also at a standstill. Over a thin veil of night-blackened trees, the buildings stand so tall and bright that even at this distance they hurt my eyes.

Clarice inches into the left lane, and much to my relief, she manages to skirt the blockage. I've been riding for so long all I can think about is getting home and getting out of the car. The minute we arrive in Ruston, I plan to toss my bags into the hallway and crawl straight into bed. I'm ready to hit the crisp sheets waiting for me back home. Damn the alarm clock, I'm going to sleep until I *feel* like getting up again.

Whenever I'm coming back from traveling east, Vicksburg is that "almost home" marker for me. I see the lights and I'm ready to be back on my own soil. Every time I reach the Mississippi River Bridge, I feel a restless stirring. It's at this point I know I'm heading into Louisiana. I'm well on my way home, just not quite there yet. I always catch myself thinking *a few more miles, only a few more miles.*

Tonight is no different.

Clarice and I had planned to make it a straight drive home from Georgia, doable with two drivers taking shifts. If the weather hasn't slowed us down too much, we should make it home shortly after midnight.

The open arch of the bridge yawns over the interstate, the frame of it resembling a large steel cage. Dozens of headlights come and go along the divided lanes. A small thrill passes through me as we leave Vicksburg.

I look for the little sign mid-bridge that announces we've crossed into Louisiana. Once I see it, I loosen my grip on the armrest and settle back into the seat, only now realizing how on edge I've been. Riding through heavy traffic sometimes does that to me.

Tonight, the muddy Mississippi comforts me. I look out the window. Lights bob on the rusty black water. Lighted riverboats are at a standstill along the east bank.

Halfway across the bridge, the lights become less visible. Darkness seeps into the car, and hard shadows pass between the steel support beams. As we drive over the bridge, wind stirred by the car rings through the steel. The tone is an eerie, hollow hum, a whispered tenor that makes me uneasy.

We make it to the opposite side of the bridge, and I let out a breath. Had I been holding it all that time? The main thing is that we've passed all the casinos and the traffic has thinned out.

After the brightness of Vicksburg, the Louisiana side of the river throws us into almost total darkness. The horizon flattens out, and as the car's headlights track a path ahead of us, a blue road sign flashes past—Welcome to Louisiana, *Bienvenue én Louisiane.*

Only a hundred miles left to go, and we'll be home.

Clarice and I spent the past week in Atlanta at a sewing and crafters' convention. While she picked out fabric and notions for her tailoring business, I stood around people watching and eating too much. That first day, I walked until my feet hurt.

In the trunk of the car, we have about twenty bolts of fabric, the cost of which still makes me wince. And in the back seat, there's a specialty sewing machine that after some heehawing about whether or not she wanted to purchase it, Clarice charged to her credit card. Three thousand dollars for a single machine.

After we left Georgia, every couple of miles Clarice would shake her head and say, "Jack is gonna kill me. You know that, don't you?"

I let her ramble, even laughed and agreed with her a time or two, but I know Jack. Granted, he'll be miffed when he sees the bill, but after his initial tantrum about finances, I expect all will be right in the world again.

By next Friday, Clarice will have those new bolts of cloth on the racks, and she'll be well on her way to having that stupid sewing machine figured out. While I'm on break between classes, she'll drag me into her sewing room and show me all the fancy things her new baby can do. My God, she'll probably want to test-embroider everything I own— and to avoid hurting her feelings, I'll probably let her.

I can't sew a stitch, and honestly, I don't care much for sewing as a task by itself. However, it means something to Clarice to teach her little sister about the inner workings of her business, so I go along with it. I show interest in it for her, which is the main reason I agreed to go on this trip in the first place. I mean, really, who even knew there was such a thing as a fabric convention?

A short distance past the welcome sign, the roads turn to shit. The smoother Mississippi asphalt trails off suddenly into Louisiana patches and pits. The first few jostle me, but after dealing with that initial stretch of bumpy road, I settle into the familiarity of it and relax again.

The scenery along the roadside is blotted out by rain and the pitch blackness of the night sky. Stalks of waist high grass jut out of the ditch. We drive through a desolate stretch of country where there isn't a business or a homestead to be seen for miles, just open fields sheltered by nightfall.

Slashing silver rain falls in the path of the headlights, and as the scenery scrolls by, the road appears suspended in empty space. There's nothing to look at, and it's easy to lose yourself in your own private thoughts. It's easy to let your imagination run away with you.

This is the closest I've been to home in days, and I think my bones must know it. I'm restless but tired at the same time.

I yawn big, and Clarice looks over at me. I say nothing and lean my seat back a bit, and my sister reaches behind me with her right hand and fishes out her coat from the floor space. She tugs it up front, and I curl up with it, the tails falling over my lap.

I turn on my side and look out at the shapeless scenery, eyes heavy and the seat belt rubbing the underside of my chin. The car dips and skates, eating up the miles. I tire of trying to hold down the shoulder strap between my chin and my shoulder so I reach down and click it off. The strap hangs slack, and I lower the seat back a little more.

Much better.

The windshield wipers beat rhythmically, back and forth. I relax and let my eyes slip shut. I've slept like this a dozen times on countless road trips.

I don't remember actually dozing off. It seems my thoughts merely skip a moment in time. Like an out-of-body experience, I'm sleeping, but awake. In my mind's eye, I'm watching the headlights push farther and farther up the road.

The car coasts over the potholes, the dips, and the ragged, rough patches of asphalt. It feels like I'm on a schooner navigating choppy seas. I'm sailing along at a fast clip, buoyant and comfortable, while dreaming about traveling to some exotic, isolated beach with crashing waves and swaying palms.

Clarice's alarmed cry startles me awake. My head in a fog, I surface from the dream, afraid, heart racing. The car fishtails, veering sharply to the left then the right. The motion throws me against the passenger door. Ahead of us, two blinding, bright circles of light appear, forcing me to squint. At that same moment, a horn blares at us, loud and urgent. The sound is right on us, threatening impact.

My heart leaps. "Clarice!"

Her responding scream dies beneath the impact, a sonic boom of metal obliterating metal. The airbags deploy in futile automation. I glimpse them, a dusty flash of white as the car crumples in on us. A sudden rush of air steals my breath. Glass shatters from all directions around us, and the cold rushes over me as I'm ejected out of the car by an invisible force. A split second later I hit the ground so hard it rattles my brain. The stillness around me is sudden and absolute.

Dizzy and disoriented, I gasp for breath and pain shrieks through my entire body. The agony is incredible. A red haze pulses before my eyes, but I fight to remain conscious, fearing what will happen to me if I don't. As the stabbing pain races along every screaming nerve ending, I struggle to catch my breath. It feels as though a boulder is crushing my chest. The need to throw up clenches my insides, but when I try to move, to roll over onto my side, I can't. My body won't obey. There's too much pain, throbbing and bone deep.

The wet, cold ground soaks into my back, and the icy wind slices into my skin. The rain comes down so hard it feels like fragments of glass peppering my face. My heart is racing, and I can see my breath frosting on the night air.

Minutes tick by. The dark emptiness of the landscape around me looks like a stage backdrop, illusory and terrifying. I know I need to move. I desperately want to find Clarice to see if she's okay, but I can't summon the strength.

My fingertips ache as if frostbitten, and a sharp pins and needles sensation tingles through my legs and arms. When I try to move this time, little lights pulse behind my eyes. I still can't seem to draw in enough air. A heavy heart beat pulses in my ears, and I know it's my own.

I stare at the indeterminable landscape until something gleaming and black steps into my view—a pair of shoes.

Oh, thank God!

My vision blurs from a sudden burst of hot tears, then an unshakeable fear blossoms in my chest. Is Clarice…dead? She has to be gravely injured, otherwise she would have coming looking for me by now. My heart breaks for her, and for my brother-in-law, Jack. What will he do when he finds out about the crash? Who'll call him to let him know? Who'll call our mother and tell her where we are?

Hot blood creeps down my scalp like a troupe of ants, persistent and itchy. My forehead stings, but I don't have the strength to reach up and touch my face.

Frightening thoughts peck at my brain. I open my mouth to speak to the man wearing those shiny black shoes, but my throat catches—wetness tickles there. I cough and blood bubbles up, thick and hot, the taste like salted iron.

My breathing quickens, and my chest grows tighter. Soon I can only draw in small, shallow breaths. Panic ripples through me, and goose bumps sheet my skin.

The man with the black shoes doesn't touch me. He doesn't try to assess my wounds in any way, and I can only beg him in my mind: *Please don't leave me. Don't let me die!*

A tide of hope washes over me when he leans down for a closer look. I'm so relieved he's here, that I'm not alone. My eyes skim his face, which is a mask of angles and shadows. His skin is marble-like in the darkness, very pale, and his straight nose and full lips give him an unnatural beauty you'd expect to find on a sculpted statue, not a living being. Dark hair hangs around his face, fringy and wet.

I keep expecting him to say something, or to assess my injuries, but he simply hovers there, staring. He makes no move to touch me. At the very least, I expect to see his mouth move, or to feel him check my pulse, but he does neither of these things. Instead, he crouches down beside me like a huge black bird and appears to wait.

I try to lift a hand to capture his, but my limbs are too stiff, too heavy to move. I'm still able to move my fingers, just barely, and I manage to brush them against his long, black coat.

He looks down at the hand touching him, and then at me, my face. He appears hesitant to respond to me, but after a few seconds, he waves a hand in front of my eyes.

Please, I try to mouth at the man. *Help me.*

His mouth draws down at the corners. Sidling closer, he studies my face and gazes into my eyes the way someone might peer into a dark window. What he's looking for, I can't imagine, but

when he passes a hand before my eyes again, this
time, I follow the motion.

His lips part slightly as if in awe. He leans
closer, almost nose to nose with me, and fear stabs
my heart. I see him clearly. His eyes—they gleam
like obsidian, cold and hard, and completely
black—no whites to them, no colored irises.
They're empty, inhuman eyes.

The way he tilts his head reminds me of a
bird of prey that has swooped down upon someone
weaker. I try to scream for help, but the sound
won't come. It's trapped inside me, locked in a
bubble of fear and anguish. A bubble of blood
lodged in my throat. I feel it squirming deep inside,
but it can't break free.

The stranger turns to me and places a finger
across my lips in a gesture of silence. Then in an
awkward, uncertain way, he touches my face. I
shiver as his ice-cold hand prods my cheekbones,
then my jaw. His thumb and pinky rest on either
side of my chin. He pinches me, prodding the flesh
along either side of my mouth. Next, he drags a
finger along the bridge of my nose. For a moment,

he pulls back completely and seems to contemplate the entire picture of my face.

Just when I think he's finished with me, he leans forward again as if in afterthought and traces a fingertip over my left eyebrow with the curious touch of someone exploring a mask.

His face twists into an expression of grim expectation, a distant, almost clinical sadness that frightens me. Apparently satisfied with whatever he has discovered, he withdraws from me again and sits down on the ground beside me.

He looks up at the drizzling sky, and all I can do is lie there and feel the cold caress of the rain tracking over my face.

Time ticks by in heartbeats. No one else has come. There are no other cars are on the road. The darkness is a suffocating blanket without the flare of oncoming headlights, and I'm alone with it, alone with the darkness and this soulless man who will not help me.

I think of my sister's voice—I need *something*, anything to comfort me, but I'm tired and growing weaker by the minute. I can barely think straight anymore. My eyelids droop, and sleep nags me. A persistent feeling of chest-gripping anxiety holds me hostage, and as futile as it seems, I know I can't afford to lose consciousness.

My breathing slows further, and I stare at the man beside me, my eyes filling with hot tears. I know in the deepest reaches of my soul that I'm dying. What's worse, I fear that is what he anticipates. That my death is what he's waiting for.

Tightness grips my lungs and holds on, and after a short time, I discover I don't need to breathe anymore.

My pulse throbs in my ears, and it's the only sound I can hear. All the noise has left the rest of the world. Even the rain falls in silence. There is only the beating of my own heart, and I hear it slowing.

Slowing.

Purple-blue blots flicker before my eyes, matching the rhythm of my pulse. The blots seem to dance across the profile of the stranger, who shuffles beside me like a bleak bird ruffling its feathers.

In my peripheral vision, a single headlight beams from an approaching vehicle. The light is weak. It falls at an angle that makes a halo around the stranger's body, and makes it appear as if there are two long, sloping shapes attached to his back. The smooth arcs start just over his head and run along the curve of his shoulders—a trick of light, surely.

Nevertheless, I imagine they are wings, rain-flecked and glistening, carved out of shadows, faded black.

Prince of Thorns

Dark waves lapped against the legs of the dilapidated fishing pier. Kane Noble stepped out onto the weathered boards, the planks shifting, groaning beneath his boots. The icy December wind gusted in from the southwest, tugging at his trench coat and sweeping his choppy brown hair away from his angular face.

Across the murky Red River, the streetlights blazed and the high-rise buildings along the boardwalk shed streaks of colored light across the stark surface of the water. Above it all, orange phosphorescence hung in the night sky over even the tallest buildings, the fiery glow reaching high to the heavens like a burning, spectral cloud.

Kane stared at the view with a grimace of detachment, his blue eyes narrowed at the hellish appearance of the sky. It reminded him of another such place, but it had been a lifetime ago that he had walked in the presence of gods.

In those long stretches of time when he existed without encountering another like himself, he could almost believe that The Fall had not happened, that he was like any other man that walked the city streets. But he wasn't human, and his knowledge of life and death went well beyond mortal understanding.

He'd once had the freedom to come and go between the various planes of existence as duty required. For untold millennia, he'd been a common witness to things human eyes and ears would struggle to comprehend. He had heard the ethereal notes of pure joy sung in a chorus of infinite voices, and had sat on the edge of the abyss while listening to the endless cries of torment. Even if it were not part of his curse to remember, he wouldn't have wanted to erase the faded memories of his origin.

Tonight the veil between the mortal realm and Oblivion seemed remarkably thin. Nights like this reminded him that in some instances angels and demons were really not all that different from mortal men.

His mouth tightened into a thin line when he thought about all he had to lose: his various real estate investments, his beloved art collection, and his latest lover, Josephine, who at twenty-four was still young and idealistic and had no clue who or what he really was.

In another time, another place, he might have thought these things trivial, but if he had learned nothing else over the course of several human lifetimes, it was that nothing remained constant. People changed, civilizations fell. You had to cherish even the basest trappings while they lasted, and when it came to living—your very existence—you had to cherish that above all else.

Every vibration felt along the celestial thread posed a threat. If one of the wise ones, the ancient angels who had succumbed to The Fall, were to track him down or trap him, they could not only take his power or his life, they could possibly bind him and keep him as a summoning slave. None of those options sounded appealing, so nothing could be left to chance. Every thread had to be traced and eliminated, including this latest one. It had taken Kane weeks to track this particular demon, and tonight he knew he was close.

Using his heightened senses, he tuned his soul to the shadows. Within seconds, a vibration of evil resonated inside him like a plucked cord. He closed his eyes and concentrated. The strength of the demon's power nearly took his breath, but he held the connection and attempted to trace the vibration back to its source.

As wave upon wave of blistering hatred reached him, dread gathered in his heart.

He recognized this power.

Kane opened his eyes, knowing what he had to do. After one last glance at the boardwalk and its shimmering reflection, he turned his back on the lights and followed the psychic trail away from the pier.

****

Kane walked for half an hour, wandering down side streets, doubling back, slipping in and out of the shadows. In a crumbling neighborhood several blocks from the riverfront, the tugging pulse of evil sharpened into an unmistakable guidepost. It led him down an empty, lamp lit street to the stoop of a crumbling brownstone. He stood in front of the building, and an ominous tension hung heavy in the air, prickling the fine hairs on the back of his neck in silent warning. He had found the right place, no doubt about that.

Undaunted, he reached inside his long, black coat and felt for the hilt of his sword then climbed the front steps and stopped where crisscrossed boards blocked off a green metal door streaked with rust. A dull throb of power emanated from the entryway—a hidden spell. Kane waved his hand in front of the door, and in the language of the Damned he muttered, *"Blood of my blood."*

Instantly, a symbol resembling a pitchfork with a crossed hilt appeared on the facing in a greasy smear of blood.

Kane recognized the unholy seal of protection for what it was and snarled under his breath. Heat flared behind his eyes, his body temperature rising with his anger. It would take more than a simple spell to keep him out.

Chanting the words that would allow him passage, he watched the symbol catch fire and burn away. When nothing remained of the seal but a blurred scorch mark, he reached through the boards for the door handle.

Triumph zinged through his veins when the door opened easily. However, as he bent to squeeze himself through the gap between the boards, what sounded like a thousand birds shot screeching from the roof. He flinched at the noise, his muscles bunching in reflex. Frozen to the spot, he glanced up, but there was no sign of any birds in the night sky. The dread he'd felt earlier clutched his heart like a vice.

He glanced across the street at the darkened tenements. Nothing moved. Perfect silence. The wind didn't even shift. It was as if the city held its breath.

Kane kept a hand on the hilt of his sword. The neighborhood appeared empty, but he knew better. He sensed someone waiting inside, someone otherworldly and powerful. Even now, the demon was probably watching him break in.

Ready to face his new enemy, he ducked through the narrow entrance into a trashed lobby. There he stood up, careful to avoid the hanging debris, the wires and tufts of insulation that dangled from the ravaged ceiling. The front lobby was divided into two long hallways with the skeletal remains of a large central staircase nestled between them. The open niche where the staircase had once stood was now piled high with broken bits of plaster, insulation, and heaps of old tile. Kane tried to scale the edge of the pile to look straight up through the hole in the ceiling, but the mountain of rubble blocked out the light and his view of the second floor.

Following the malevolent vibration, he took a chance and started down the right-side hallway. Midway down, a huge graffiti arrow on an intact stretch of wall within the gutted corridor pointed him onward. Even when light at both ends of the corridor narrowed into distant squares, he continued toward the back of the building.

Minutes later, he emerged into a small, rear lobby where blanched moonlight fell in broken diamond patterns through a trio of tall square windows covered by a protective grate. Beside the windows, a thick metal door with a push bar had been secured by a heavy chain to prevent anyone from getting in, or getting out.

Kane studied the patterns of light for a long moment, searching for the psychic threads of a trap. When he was sure there were none, he continued forward. To his left, tucked away in a shadowy corner, he found a damp, carpeted stairway leading up to the second floor.

Air flowed from the upper levels, the faint breeze reeking of mildew and the sweetness of death. Here the psychic vibration thickened until it became almost unbearable. Kane gritted his teeth against the throbbing in his temples and rounded a sagging wooden banister, eyeing the black mold clinging to the staircase wall like spots of disease.

The stairs led up two flights to an open floor sectioned off by ancient scaffolding and clear plastic sheeting that had likely been tacked up to keep and dust or rain out of the abandoned work areas.

Kane realized the interior wasn't especially large, but rather the second and third floors had been completely gutted up to the bare bones of the roof. The night sky was visible through the ceiling where holes the size of bowling balls spilled inward like ragged wounds.

He lingered near the entrance, his heart pounding, his breath frosting in and out on the icy air. The grim surroundings put him on edge when he recognized this place for what it was: he had inadvertently stumbled upon someone's lair. No telling how long the source of power had lived here, but it was clear the building had been in a state of disrepair for a very long time. Along the outer walls and throughout the entire floor, the abandoned metal scaffolding had rusted in place, creating a kind of unintentional maze that made it impossible to see from one end of the floor to another.

Looking for signs of life, he carefully scanned the beams and the hidden recesses, but the only movement seemed to come from a phantom breeze that occasionally gained enough strength to rustle the sheets of plastic.

When at last Kane shifted from the doorway into a patch of protective shadows, he stepped into a pool of something dark and sticky on the floor. Frowning, he lifted his foot from it, and the coppery fragrance of blood stirred in the air, wafting up to him like stale, pungent spice.

His mouth twisted into a grimace. He moved deeper into the heart of the room, careful to avoid the plastic sheeting and the possibility that he might unintentionally reveal himself in the patches of moonlight from the high, square windows along the outer walls.

At the base of one scaffold, two large wet drops fell from somewhere high and landed on his cheek. Kane flinched as it hit him then wiped at the wetness and looked at his hand. Blood, cold and thick as oil, smeared his fingers.

Heart hammering, he stepped back into beneath a crooked platform and glanced up toward the roof. Above him, lodged high in the rafters, a shadowed heap darkened the crux of two beams. A human hand dangled over the edge into moonlit view, a black runnel of liquid streaking down the heel of the palm.

He curled his lips in distaste, and called out into the silence. "Come out, Nepali. I know it's you. I would recognize your stench anywhere."

Above him the shadows shifted, and the sound of rustling wings settled somewhere nearby. The offended demon had been roosting in the rafters the entire time. After a moment the fluttering stopped and Kane heard a loud twisting noise, like talons digging deep into wood. He pulled his sword quietly from the scabbard, expecting an attack at any moment.

"You tread on my territory, Kane," an inhuman voice croaked. "What brings you to my lair?"

"I sensed your presence and came looking for you."

Nepali scoffed. "I hope you're not one of those weeping sentimentalists. As you can see, I'm hardly set up to entertain guests."

"It doesn't matter," Kane assured him. "I don't intend to stay long."

"How polite of you," the demon said with a hideous chuckle. "Forgive me if I am not a gracious host."

"I understand—it's nothing personal."

"Oh, but it is. You've come to destroy me. I'd say that's intensely personal."

"If that's how you wish to take it…" Kane stepped into the light, a silent challenge for Nepali to do the same.

A loud shriek like the cawing of a crow sent gooseflesh chasing over Kane's arms and down his back. He ducked down as once again Nepali swooped through the rafters in a fit of rustling wings that stirred the plastic barriers. Kane braced himself for the coming battle. More than likely, the decrepit wise one was searching out a better vantage point to launch his attack.

The demon landed with a clatter somewhere among the groaning maze of scaffolding a few feet away. Through the shadows and the sheeting, Kane could just make out Nepali's form crouched atop a low platform. He looked monstrous: a ratted mop of hair, a white limbed body dressed in shabby coattails that draped down like the folded wings of a bat.

Nepali's voice thickened as he chanted a series of harsh guttural curses in the old language, words promising vengeance and the agony of death. As he spoke, his eyes took on a red, reflective glow. They were the eyes of a very old man, or perhaps those of a dead man. Kane decided Nepali hadn't taken very good care of himself in his fleshly form.

Outside, the wind lifted in response to the evil spell. It howled like a tormented soul as it caressed the corners of the tenement and slipped invisible fingers into the building through the many holes and crags. A pressure built up in the room, and the celestial thread hummed with violent tension.

The fallen one finished off his string of curses by tracing a symbol of death into the air. Garnet flames flickered for a brief moment before the spell vanished, a hidden trap lying in wait. It was then Nepali stepped from the rafters and floated down, the scent of disease and decay wafting from his unclean body. He whipped out a long curved blade a scant second before his taloned feet touched the floor. In a quick show of mastery, he slashed the blade through the air before settling into a defensive stance.

Kane lifted his own sword in answer.

Red-rimmed eyes glowed in the shadowed face of his opponent. Nepali held out his arms as if to embrace a long lost friend, the head of ratted hair tilted to the side in a gesture of confusion. "Why have you come for me, Kane? Whatever have I done to you?"

"This is my city. I'm merely clearing out the attic."

Nepali shrieked with rage.

"I will not be moved," Kane shouted over the demon's bleating. "Your presence poses a danger to me, old friend. Your lair is too close to my resting place."

"Arrogant prick!" Nepali's voice boomed. He paced with his sword at the ready, preparing to strike. "I won't allow you to chase me from my home."

"We shall see, won't we?"

"Oh, we will see, *my prince*," Nepali sneered, his words followed by a hideous, clucking laugh that sounded like a hundred voices overlaid in horrific concert. "Long gone are the days of honor and duty. You no longer have the power to command me. There are no titles among us in this land of rot!"

Before Kane could blink, Nepali lunged at him, the sound of his fast-forward movement like a flock of birds taking sudden flight. The demon struck out at him with short, determined flicks of the sword. Sparks flashed off metal as Kane parried each rapid strike.

Sword crashed against sword. Every powerful blow radiated up Kane's arm. Nepali's skill had not diminished over the ages. Kane grimaced as the demon's blade slid down the length of his own sword with a ringing metallic sound and caught him at the hilt. He shoved the demon off before his sword could be plucked away from his grasp. *Tricky.* He barely managed to resume his stance before Nepali lunged at him yet again.

The two warriors twirled and paced, lashing out at one another in a fierce dance of skill and hatred. Kane moved under one of the scaffolds to avoid a blow, but Nepali's blade made contact with an odd clang and severed the rusted metal at the joint. The razor edge caught Kane's coat in the process and sliced easily through the fabric. He jumped back, but not before the blade nicked the flesh of his left arm.

He snarled at the raw, stinging pain. The celestial thread that tethered them together cried out in a warbling, high pitch note that rang so loudly it seemed to shiver through him body and soul.

A surge of panic washed through Kane as blood flowed freely down his arm. Power crackled in the air, intensified by his fear and anger. He thought of his black haired Josephine waiting at home in his comfortable bed and a sick feeling of anticipation rooted low in his belly. He wondered absently if it were true what the old wives said about the portent of death—that a man's life often flashed before his eyes right before he died.

Nepali fell back into a defensive stance and cackled. "Looks like I score first blood, *Your Highness*." He gave a mock bow, but Kane would not be goaded.

Instead, he braced himself for the next wave of attack. Nepali advanced quickly then retreated in what Kane suspected was an attempt to throw him off balance. To his frustration, it was working. Winded, his wound throbbing, he focused on his opponent and waited for an opportunity to lash out.

At last it came. Nepali had forced him back almost to the mouth of the stairwell when suddenly he charged forward in a burst of movement that blurred into shadow. Kane reacted rather than thought. With a roar of determination, he pivoted out of the way and struck blindly with his blade. The demon couldn't have seen it coming. Kane barely had time to process his own actions when the sword caught Nepali at the base of his throat, slicing through the gray flesh.

Kane felt a flash of excruciating pain as the celestial thread snapped. With a bark of alarm, he tugged his sword free of the wound. Nepali's pained smile instantly faded. The demon made a gurgling, sputtering sound, as he stumbled to his knees. Standing off to the side, Kane was stunned to silence by the look of shock and terror glittering the Nepali's eyes. Worse than that, the light from the rear lobby illuminated his old friend's face. He was right. He did remember him, albeit vaguely. The former archangel looked barely recognizable, nothing at all like a glorious being Kane remembered from the time before The Fall. Instead, Nepali looked much like a melted candle. Bulbous rolls of sagging flesh hung from the heavily scarred cheeks, jowls, and the newly slashed throat.

Nepali's last words were a gurgled eulogy uttered as he slumped forward into a heap and was still. Oily blood flowed from the wound, pooling away from the body as if trying to escape the corruption of the physical form. Kane watched without moving until the blood flowed over the edge of the top stair, the trajectory gone from his view.

He lowered his sword. Strangely enough, the vibration of evil ebbed, but it didn't go away entirely. It took him several moments to realize that he still felt a pulse of some demonic connection. It should have died with Nepali.

Wary, watching for a trap, he scanned the shadows, looking for others. Demons didn't normally congregate together, but he supposed it wasn't impossible.

He didn't return his attention to Nepali's corpse until he was convinced there were no others in the immediate vicinity. Several minutes had passed before he walked over to the shriveling corpse and frowned down at the fallen soldier.

Although he was certain he had known Nepali well in the past, when he tried to remember the finer details of their friendship, or anything specific about the time they might've spent in duty side by side, the memories eluded him.

Nevertheless, a feeling of sadness clutched at his heart. A frown creased his brow as he passed his hand over the prone body and offered up the death chant to release the demon's immortal spirit from this plane.

"I cast you into Oblivion where you belong," he chanted in the old language.

He traced the symbol of eternity into the air, and it caught fire, flickering a brief moment before fading to black. The scent of death and brimstone blossomed in the room, and at once Nepali's body began to sizzle. The ruined clothes caught fire, the flames spreading rapidly over the ravaged body. Within minutes, nothing remained but a blackened, shriveled shell that flattened out further and further until the cleansing fire reduced him to ashes, both inside and out. Kane's mouth tightened into a thin line. *"May eternal torment greet you, my brother."*

By morning, nothing would remain of Nepali but a memory. A vague one at that. Kane was both saddened and relieved.

His task complete, he turned away from the remains and wiped his sword on one of the plastic sheets before sliding it back into the rosewood scabbard. Then for a long moment afterward he stood weighing the silence and marveling at his own stark awareness of Nepali's death.

Strangely enough, it felt as though something inexplicably important had been plucked from the world, and that an indefinable sense of purpose had been lost to him forever. He couldn't explain it and didn't try. Kane had felt a twinge of this before when he had killed other demons, but admittedly, the feeling had never cut him as deeply as it did now.

His boots thudded over the hardwood floor as he made his way toward the center of the scaffolding maze. There, moonlight beamed down, creating a circular patch of blue-white brightness. It looked almost like a spotlight. Kane stepped into the circle of light and looked up, studying the ceiling before leaping up into the rafters and climbing out through the hole in the roof.

Outside, the midnight breeze smelled dusty and damp, like sidewalks after a summer rain. The flat roof matched the rest of the building. It had been abandoned without repair. From the look of it, the owners must've realized they'd need more than a few buckets of roofing tar, asphalt fabric, and piles of roofing gravel to save this place.

Watching his step, Kane found a secure looking section of the roof and dropped to his knees. He felt light-headed, and the slash wound on his arm throbbed with raw pain. He rolled his neck and took a deep breath. He held it for a long moment before exhaling slowly. Closing his eyes, he waited for his head to clear, but as soon as he relaxed enough to push away the pain, he picked up on the faint psychic vibration of another demon.

He frowned. Was it perhaps a matter of karmic gravity that drew the fallen ones to one another? An otherworldly example of the law of attraction—like drawn to like?

He'd probably never know the answer.

Eyes watering from the frosty bite of the wind, he eased his arm out of his coat to assess the damage Nepali had done to his arm. His skin was stained crimson from the blood he'd lost. While the wound had crusted over, it was still raw. It would likely take a good hour before the wound sealed itself shut.

Although he healed faster than a mortal man, he couldn't rush the process. The wound would probably be healed over by the time he made it home, but his blood stained skin and clothes would not be easy to hide from his human mate— his wife—Josephine.

For several minutes he debated sending Josephine a text message to let her know he would be home late. It would buy him extra time to make his way out to one of the truck stops on I-20 so he could shower before heading home.

He felt in his pocket for his cell phone, but hesitated as the faint wave of power he'd felt only moments ago intensified. Dread coiled in his stomach. It was the same psychic connection he'd felt only moments after he had killed Nepali. Definitely another demon, but was it closer than he thought?

With considerable effort, he rose to his feet and walked to the edge of the building. There he crouched down, his boots crunching over the pea-sized gravel. Honing in on the phantom vibration, he squinted off into the distance, at the view of the towering rose lights glowing along Riverfront Park. He cursed under his breath. Unless he was mistaken, the trail of psychic energy came from somewhere in the direction of his lair, off by no less than perhaps a few miles.

Coincidence? Or was someone hunting him the way he had hunted Nepali?

Somehow the idea of being hunted didn't surprise him that much. Given the circumstances, Kane guessed it had always been only a matter of time.

One thing for certain, he had no intention of giving up or running away. He was driven to survive, to continue to exist. As Josephine would say, he had to keep on keeping on. It was as good advice as any.

With a new resolve to protect himself and his territory, Kane locked onto this new path of evil and floated down from the rooftop to the street below.

The Last Words of Paul Odom

One

I haven't rested well in days. There's so much on my mind, so many things to sort out. I figure the only way to make sense of it is to write it down. Might as well, since there's no one left to talk to.

Sometimes when I'm downstairs, I pick up the telephone and talk into the line. There's no dial tone anymore, so it's easy to imagine someone is listening. My nerves are so shot sometimes just talking aloud makes me feel better, even if only for a little while.

I live in the constant fear that one of those things will break into the house while I'm sleeping. Last week I moved everything I need on a day-to-day basis into the attic, and now I only go downstairs during the day. Even then, I sometimes hear scuffling noises outside the house, but I never know for sure if what I'm hearing is real or imagined. The doors are locked and barricaded, and I try to avoid peeking out the windows if I can help it. It's best not to get too curious about what goes on out there.

So far, no one has tried to break in. I'm not sure if it's because everyone is too far gone to remember how to break in a window, or because the house looks like a dead zone not worthy of investigation. Maybe it's a little of both. After what I've seen, I'm cautious when I go downstairs or outside to find supplies, especially since I don't know what the fresher ones are capable of.

Two

At night, I barricade myself into the attic by pulling up the folding stairs and shoving my great grandmother's armoire over the hatch. During the daylight hours, I go downstairs, check the doors and windows, and fill up all the spare buckets and jugs with water to haul back up to the attic. I live in fear that the water will get turned off, or the water will simply run out, or that the main will burst and the water won't make it out this far. If that happens, I'll have to walk a quarter of a mile to Johnson's creek to find fresh water, and I'd rather avoid that if I can help it.

The house is safe enough for now, but it's hard to look at the place when I leave the attic. All the life and joy has bled out of it. It's a shelter, no longer a home. The house feels dead inside, as if it has been abandoned for a hundred years. The miserable weather isn't helping matters, either. The August heat is uncomfortable well before eleven in the morning, and by one o'clock in the afternoon, it's stifling hot. The electricity went out two weeks ago, and without lights and air conditioning, the house is miserable and humid. Around midday, I often lie on the floor without a shirt and wonder if the heat of the closed up house is enough to bake me alive.

Most days, I try to go through my daily routine on autopilot, since the slightest thing can trigger a bone deep sense of loss that damn near sends me over the edge. Like last week, when I saw the handmade throw pillows in the den, or the time I noticed Susanna's tulip print apron hanging on a peg by the back door. The other day I saw her toothbrush standing in the ceramic cup by the bathroom sink, and I lost it. Just like that, I broke down sobbing. And I couldn't stop myself. I cried in gut-wrenching anguish for a good thirty minutes, until finally I had to crouch down in front of the toilet and throw up.

Three

Her cries for me never cease. If I stand on the back porch, I can hear her clearly—Susanna, my wife. Somehow, she is still alive in the dark depths of the well in our backyard. Each note is wounded and raw, the sound of a desperate, starving animal. What's worse, there are times the rise and fall of the wind carries the sounds up to the house. I swear it's true. Even in the attic, I can hear the throaty moans. Late at night, they taper away in a strange guttural clacking that sounds like dried leaves rattling on the branches of a dead tree.

It seems impossible, I know. The well itself is seventy-five feet deep, with only a splash of water left in the bottom. The Shively township water table has been low for years, and until last summer, there was enough water to use the well for our vegetable garden, or to wash the dust off my old farm truck.

I cringe whenever I imagine her wading knee deep in the cold darkness, her fingers raking the stone walls. The nightmare image is burned into my brain, haunting me whether I'm awake or dreaming.

I've never shown a light down the well to check for sure that she is still trying to reach me. Do the dead give up when they are trapped? Do they keep going until the flesh and muscle rots away? I don't know how I'd take it if I looked down the well and saw Susanna looking up at me with undead eyes. What she must look like now after being stuck in the water for this long… It's probably for the best I don't know.

Four

It's the middle of the night. Maybe an hour ago, I woke up sobbing from a nightmare. I dreamed I was lost, stumbling in the dark, and although I couldn't see it, I knew it was there—a hole in the ground waiting to swallow me up. Dry, clacking moans echoed all around me, and the wind was bitterly cold. I tried to wrap my arms around myself to warm up, but the suit I wore had a giant split up the back.

Five

My greatest fear is that I'll forget them— Susanna and Alison. I try to remember their smiles but death floats before my eyes instead. It's torture remembering them, but it feels like I'm betraying their memory if I don't think about them every moment of every day.

Whenever I'm downstairs, I stare at their pictures, the big ones on the mantle in the living room. I want to burn those images into memory, lodge the details so deep I can never forget, but when I look away from their pictures even for an instant, the fantasy comes crashing down around me.

If they were truly dead, I believe it would be easier to make peace. Maybe then I could accept they're gone. Instead, I hear them crying out to me, and I have to keep reminding myself they're not the people in the pictures anymore.

Six

How it began. I think I can talk about it now. I've started to write about it several times, but I always…I don't know. I choke up. The words are there, but I struggle to get them out. Tears come instead. Despair descends on me like a dark cloud, but I need to talk about it. The memories are demons I need to exorcise.

I'm not entirely sure what the date is. The days and nights blur together. I believe it's late September, but there's no way to know for sure. Months ago, back in April, Susanna and I celebrated eleven years of marriage. Alison had just turned six months old, and we were excited that she had started to sit up by herself. Susanna's younger brother, Miguel, who has lived with us ever since we got married, turned nineteen, and only a few weeks before, he'd moved into a travel trailer we'd set up for him on a half-acre plot near the barns. We did this to give him his privacy, even though he still spent most of his time at the house with us. We were happy, doing well. We were content with life and with each other. Then the world changed.

I still don't know what brought it on, but it seemed to happen overnight. The news didn't hint of any coming apocalypse, but one morning, toward the end of June, I drove the tractor out front to get a start on the mowing. I'd cut maybe a half acre when I noticed someone standing off in the distance. It was a man in a dark suit. The sun was bright that day, the weather unseasonably hot. I sat on the tractor watching him, waiting to see him move. It was impossible to guess what he was doing. He was just standing there in the field in front of the house, looking out toward Harper Road.

I stopped Old Blue and sat for a long minute, squinting, occasionally wiping the sweat out of my eyes. I glanced over my shoulder, wondering if I should go back and call the sheriff. Susanna must've heard the tractor idling. She'd opened the front door and was watching me through the screen. She was barefoot, her long black hair caught up in a messy bun, bouncing Alison on her hip.

I took off my straw hat long enough to wipe my forehead then I put the tractor in gear and drove further down the field. I got within twenty feet of the man and killed the engine. Old Blue is noisy, but the man never once moved. He never glanced my direction, never acknowledged he heard the tractor.

The hay was so tall it brushed the man's thighs. The wind tugged at his clothes, making it appear as though he swayed slightly in the shifting wind. Wary and growing impatient, I called out to him, "Hey, mister!"

Dread crept up my spine. He hadn't made a move yet, but there was something threatening about his silence.

I thought about cranking up Old Blue and taking the tractor a shade closer, but I decided against it. I figured if the man needed help I could get Miguel to come around and move the tractor back over to the barn for me.

When I stepped down into the field, I took the short handled sling blade I keep on the tractor for whacking down creeper vines that sometimes try to take over the backyard. Blade in hand, I walked toward the man.

As I got closer, I noticed the back of his black suit had a fine rip up the back, right along the seam. When the wind blew, the fabric parted slightly, and I could see the navy fabric of a dress shirt underneath. His dark brown hair looked scraggly thin. White whorls of scalp showed through the oiled hair, but otherwise he was clean cut. Though I couldn't see his face, I knew something was very wrong with him. Fear trickled through me, and I heeded it. I stopped three feet away from him and flexed my fingers around the handle of the sling blade.

"Mister," my voice sounded strained, even to my own ears. "Do you need some kind of help?"

All I really wanted to know was what he was doing in my field. How the hell had he gotten this far out without a car? We are fourteen miles outside of Shively, and somehow I didn't think he'd gotten lost out here on his own. Wild scenarios played in my mind as I stood there. Maybe someone had kidnapped him and set him loose. Maybe someone had robbed him, dumped him in the field, and left him for dead. Regardless of how he'd landed himself here, I was hesitant to approach him. A gut deep sense of revulsion held me back.

He didn't respond to any of my attempts to talk to him, so I went around him, thinking I might get a response if I looked him in the eye. When I saw the chewed up face and the white, pasted-over eyes, I stumbled back in horrified disbelief. The man was unquestionably dead. His lips were missing. His blue-gray gums were visible and his teeth were dirty. They were crooked and yellowy, two rows of bald snappers resembling dentures set in that husk of a face. A dry raspy noise clicked in his throat, and as his blanched gaze settled on mine, he lifted an arm and shambled toward me.

Instinct took over. Blind with fear, I struck out at him. I wasn't aiming at any part of him in particular. The sling blade lodged in his skull and stuck there, and the man went down hissing and twitching in the grass. It stunned me how fast he crumpled, and I goggled at the clotted black blood oozing from the wound I'd made.

I barely remember hopping back on the tractor, but I drove Old Blue fast as she would move until I finally reached the house. Susanna rushed off the porch. "Jesus, what happened? You hit him—with the blade!"

"Get in the house!" I shouted at her.

Susanna flinched at the tone of my voice. I'd never yelled at her before. I guess Alison sensed something was up. She started bawling. I ushered them both into the house and slammed the front door, locking it behind me. Through the glass panel on the door, I looked where the man had fallen, and I could still see the wood handle of the sling blade sticking up. Then I remembered—Miguel. I pushed my way around Susanna and the baby and headed to the gun cabinet.

Susanna trailed behind me. "That man... What was wrong with him?"

"I don't know. Stay inside and call the sheriff. I have to check on Miguel." I'd last seen him earlier that morning outside the barn.

I pulled my best hunting rifle out of the gun cabinet and checked to see if it was loaded. It was. I took a handful of shells from the shelf inside and stuffed them in my pockets.

On my way out of the house, I kissed Susanna, who was rambling off all the reasons I should stay, and then I leaned over and kissed Alison's downy head. Tired and teething, she clung to her mother and continued her confused, stop-start crying. The last thing I saw before I turned away from them both was Alison's pearly baby teeth. They were two, tiny, perfectly formed nubs front and center in her lower gums. Instantly I thought of the dead man outside. I pictured his vile, blood-grooved teeth and a shiver rolled through me. The rotting chemical stench of him was still caught up my nose.

Seven

Around the perimeter of the house, the hydrangeas were in full bloom. Bees buzzed flower to flower. We had planted the bushes not long after my mother had passed away, some ten years ago. I thought of her now as I headed toward the barns.

I was shaking all over, and I was hyper aware of every little motion, every noise. I flinched at the sheets flapping on the clothesline. It had only begun to sink in that I'd just cut a man down in front of the house.

"Miguel!" I shouted across the yard. No one answered. There was no sign of him anywhere. The barn is an open shelter, a place to park the tractor and store bales of hay during the seasons we decide to keep a cow or two. When the front and back doors are open, you can see directly through the shadowy bay, end to end, and all the way to the tree line behind the building.

At first glance, I didn't see anyone in the barn, so I looked off toward my left, to the front door of Miguel's silver travel trailer. I saw it was closed and relief poured through me. I thought for sure that was where he'd gone.

I started away from the quiet, open mouth of the barn when I heard a loud snapping noise. I stopped short and glanced back. I lifted my rifle and returned to the open bay. This time, I scanned the bay from corner to corner. Across the barn, behind a stack of hay bales, I could see someone's back—it wasn't Miguel's. It was a stranger, a man, in a denim shirt that stretched taut across his broad shoulders. He was on his knees in the dirt, and I could hear faint slurping noises. Like jelly being squished between someone's fingers.

"Hey!"

The man didn't acknowledge me. Hands clutching the gun tight, I walked cautiously into the barn. When I was maybe six feet away from the man, I halted in mid step. He wasn't alone. He was leaned over Miguel's twitching body.

I don't know what I did that finally alerted the stranger to my presence. Maybe my nearness triggered it. Whatever the case, the man turned and hissed at me. Dead eyes full of hate glared at me.

I shot the bastard in the head, and he went down. When he had stopped twitching, I nudged him with my foot and he slumped over, away from the body he'd been feasting on—Miguel's. What was left of him. His throat was gone, and his face had been half eaten off. I left him there, and backed away, tears stinging my eyes and bile burning in my throat. I didn't want to have to explain this to Susanna. Hell, I didn't know if I'd be able to. I had no idea what was going on my damn self.

On my way back to the house, I noticed more people had shambled into the field. They were blood drenched. They all looked as if they had survived a brutal attack. There were two young men in jeans and T-shirts, and a woman in a pink sweatshirt with bright colored patches sewn on the front of it. They appeared to have drifted in from the direction of the town, but I have no way of knowing for sure.

While they were still a good distance away from the house, I took aim and began to pick them off one by one. I started with the woman. The first shot hit her in the shoulder. She staggered on her feet, but she seemed otherwise unfazed. I shot her again, this time in the head. She dropped like a sack of lead into the grass and didn't get up again.

Eight

Susanna turned ghostly pale when I told her about Miguel. I think she anticipated it. Without saying a word, she left me standing in the den and went to the kitchen to finish washing dishes. It was only after several minutes that she began to sob quietly.

That night, it was awful. Too quiet. There was nothing on the radio or the TV, just the emergency broadcast signal for hours on end. No news to clue us in on what had happened to cause the dead to attack us, and whether anyone was out there trying to do anything about it. Nothing to give us any hope that the world would turn right again, or that we would be rescued.

The wind lilted outside, carrying odd noises with it. Moans and shuffling sounds. We put in one of the baby's naptime sounds CDs and turned the volume low. It was better that way, to listen to the exaggerated sound of crickets, the soft ocean waves, then a rain shower than to hear the eerie sounds of the creatures outside.

On and off Susanna would cry, and despite being dog tired, I couldn't rest. The minute I closed my eyes, Miguel's mangled body came into focus. Every shifting wind and shuffling sound outside the house had me on high alert. Before we left the den and settled in for the night, we hung blankets over the windows and put the bedside lamp on the floor to keep the lights from being seen by anyone lurking outside. We then barricaded the bedroom door and windows with the heaviest pieces of furniture we own. The room was secure as we could make it. But even with Alison nestled safely between us, we slept fitfully.

The next morning, I woke up startled to find both Alison and Susanna gone. I bounded downstairs calling their names. Alison looked up at me from the playpen, but Susanna wasn't watching her. The front door was wide open, and a shriek of panic washed over me.

I rushed to the front door and peered through the screen. "Susanna!"

She was roughly twenty feet away in the front yard and still walking. Her back was to me, but I could see she had her arm up as if she were shading her eyes. My heart leapt in fear when I saw what—or rather, *whom*—she was looking at.

A man in denim shirt seemed to sway in the breeze. His hair was long and black hair like Susanna's. I was so stunned to see him there. Miguel. Less than twenty-four hours ago, I'd seen him dead, his throat ripped out.

"Susanna, no!"

She was too close to him, like I had been when I'd approached the stranger roaming the field. I leapt the porch rail and dashed across the yard toward my wife. But I was too late. Susanna laid a hand on Miguel's arm. When he turned around, giving her a full view of his shredded face and gaping throat, she screamed.

Miguel grabbed her by the shoulders, trapping her long hair beneath a rotted hand. Within seconds, he was pulling her toward him.

Susanna screamed and fought against him. I roared in fury and broadsided Miguel. I took him down like a hyped-up linebacker. Through it all, his jaws snapped open and closed as if on a hinge.

Dead, sightless eyes gazed up at me. He very nearly sank his teeth into my chest before I snatched up a chunk of old brick that had once lined the rose beds and used it to bash his head in.

The hell we went through that morning will haunt me for the rest of my life. I'd practically raised that boy. Miguel was a good kid, like a son to me. He was a hard worker. Didn't have a mean bone in his body. Whatever caused this, whatever kind of plague this was, the thing that attacked my wife that day was no longer the Miguel I knew and loved.

Susanna had great long scratches down her arms and across her neck where Miguel had tried to bite her. They looked like superficial wounds to me, but we wanted to be safe. After she took a scalding hot shower and changed into fresh clothes, we used peroxide, alcohol, and iodine on every scratch and bruise before wrapping her wounds in gauze.

Later on that evening, she was still shaken and grieving, but physically speaking, she seemed okay. She went through her usual routine, taking care of the house, taking care of Alison. But once the sun went down, melancholy settled over her. She sat silently at the kitchen table with her elbows on the tabletop. Her eyes were far away and tears streamed down her face.

Before bed, I made her a hot cup of tea and brought her a couple of antibiotics I'd found in an old prescription bottle in the master bathroom. I didn't know what else to do for her. After I'd taken care of Susanna, I picked up Alison out of her playpen, changed her diaper, and gave her a bottle to quiet her. Reluctantly, she took it. Poor girl, she was as tired and grumpy as the rest of us.

Nine

The next morning, we woke to find the power had gone out. I tried to call the sheriff again, but this time when I picked up the phone there was no dial tone, just a static clicking noise. I told Susanna I planned to go into town to see what I could find out.

Susanna didn't want me to go. She worried about us being separated, unable to reach each other, but I was determined to make the drive. I kept thinking in terms of disaster preparedness. What if we'd missed vital instructions? What if we were only supposed to be drinking bottled water? How would we know for sure unless I went out there and tried to find out what the hell was going on?

We argued, and what's really bad about it is that the whole time we fought my main concern was that I was burning daylight. She didn't want me to go alone, and I understood that. But my mind was set. Eventually she gave in and agreed to stay behind with the doors locked. She was still mad at me, but on my way out the door, I made her swear one thing: if I didn't come back by sunset, she wasn't supposed to come looking for me. Not for any reason.

I set out at ten in the morning, and I got as far as Keaton Road before the signs of disaster became truly apparent. I could see the highway from there, the way the cars were strewn like so much litter. Black smoke rose from a dozen small fires. Shively looked like a war zone.

As I drove through town, there was no sign of life. Bodies lay scattered in the streets, decomposing, food for scavenger birds—and God only knew what else. Windows were shattered and smeared with blood. Doors were ripped off the hinges. The police station looked abandoned.

I made one pass through town without stopping anywhere, and then I turned my truck around. The town was dead. That was all I needed to know. There was no other news to be found out here.

It was on my mind to grab supplies before I headed home, but everything looked ransacked and dark. Most of the larger stores appeared too dangerous to enter. I was also wary of leaving the truck unattended. Every dark window I drove past made me long for shelter. I didn't see a soul in town, but I felt hateful, hungry eyes watching me from every shadow.

I took an alternate route home. On the way out of town, I pulled over at Tammy's Eagle Stop. I used to stop there every morning for a coffee refill back when I worked at the glass plant over in Freemont. I was familiar with the layout of the

Eagle Stop—the arrangement of the shelves, and where the bathrooms were located.

The little gas station looked nearly unrecognizable. Looters had trashed the place. The windows were shattered, and the glass door, its metal frame bent, hung on by a hinge. Litter was scattered everywhere. I left the truck idling and approached cautiously with my rifle at the ready. Through the broken windows and the open entryway, I could see the business from end to end. No undead. No one at all. I quickly grabbed whatever I could find. I took what was left of the boxed food and tin cans. Three rolls of toilet paper. A bag of diapers. Bars of soap. Jugs of bleach. If it looked useful, I tossed it into the back of the truck. There'd be time to sort it out later.

I reached home in the early afternoon. I'd only been gone a few hours. Three, maybe four? I parked the truck near the side door, which is closest to the kitchen, and as I began to bring in the stuff I'd looted from Tammy's, I realized Susanna hadn't come to the door to greet me.

A feeling like spider's legs tingled along my spine. I called out to Susanna, but she didn't answer me. I stepped into the house and looked around the kitchen, the dining room. I peered into the den and kept moving. I didn't see any signs of a scuffle, but the house was strangely quiet. I wasn't sure what had happened while I was away, but I knew in my heart something had gone terribly wrong.

I wished I'd brought the gun inside with me, but it was still on the seat of the truck, so I picked up an iron bookend from the hall table as I cautiously approached the back door, which was hanging wide open. My mind desperately tried to make sense of what I was seeing, to put all the pieces together. Was she hiding somewhere with Alison? Had someone dropped by needing help? Had she let in a stranger? Had more of the dead come onto the property while I was away?

Where the hell are you?

I stepped out onto the back porch. The wind twirled the plastic garden flowers sticking up in the yard. *Click-clack, click-clack.* Someone was out there. I couldn't see them, but I felt their presence.

Dead eyes watched me from the woods, making my skin itch. I looked toward the garden shed and the wood line at the back of the property, but no one was there.

I left the back porch and walked around to the other side the house. A nagging fear had taken hold of me. I worried she had walked out to the barns. For what, I couldn't imagine, but grisly thoughts had begun to swirl in my head.

I'd just cleared the back yard when I spotted her. My heart kicked into a gallop, and I started shaking. She was standing near the well, as if she had tried to walk away from the house, but the well had been in her way. I let the bookend fall from my hand.

"Susanna." I tried to call to her, but my voice cracked. I knew before I even saw her face. The way she swayed on her feet. The lank arms and downward tilt of her head.

Tears ached in my throat. It seemed as though she had been trying to leave the house, maybe to protect me, I don't know. I walked toward her. I'm not sure what I intended to do. It just seemed the most natural thing in the world to go to her. My feet moved me forward. I'd gone lightheaded, and I felt weightless and cold.

I stopped maybe four feet away from her. I'm not sure she ever would've noticed me if I hadn't approached her. I called her name.

It took her a moment to turn and face me. Her motions were stiff and stop-start. Except for her jaundiced eyes, she looked exactly the same as she had when I'd left her that morning. Then she hissed at me, and I saw blood stained the grooves between her teeth. Her hands curled into claws, and she reached out for me. There were bite marks all along her arms—her own bite marks. She shambled forward, and the world blurred around me. Too many sounds and colors to process. My wife... When she was close enough, she snatched at the front of my shirt.

We struggled together for the barest moment, then I shoved her so hard, she fell back in a flurry of arms and plunged into the well.

The well had run dry years ago. There's barely three feet of water left at the bottom of it now. When she struck bottom, the splash sounded as if it came from miles below the earth, from the bowels of a deep cavern. No telling how long I stood there. Numb inside, I turned and looked at the house.

Then I remembered—Alison!

I glanced around the yard, but there was no sign Susanna had been carrying her. Maybe Susanna had sensed herself turning and left the house, fearing she would harm the baby. I rushed into the house, panicked, sobbing. I choked down great gulps of air. I expected to find her mangled and—I don't know. I just don't know. There were too many horrible possibilities. The blood I'd seen on Susanna's lips and teeth filled my head with dark visions. Even now, those visions make me cringe. To my relief, when I found her, she was lying on her belly in her playpen in the bedroom. She looked as perfect as she had that morning when I'd left. She was clean and intact. Whole.

She was still dressed her kitty cat pajamas and a pair of fuzzy pink crib socks, but when I leaned down and touched her back, she was cold and unmoving. I pulled back and paced. Raged. Madness gripped me. I tugged at my hair until my scalp bled, and I can't remember all the curses I shouted up to God. I bit my fist and paced. I couldn't wrap my mind around it. If Susanna hadn't harmed her, how could she be dead?

As if in a dream, I sat heavily into the rocking chair in the corner and stared at her in shock. Tears streamed down my face. A long time had passed before I noticed the bottle of breast milk in the bottom of the playpen with her. The power was out, so the milk had to be fresh. Susanna had probably expressed milk into a bottle shortly after I'd left.

The realization settled in, and I began to weep. Deep, soul wracking sobs that shook my whole body. It was then Alison started to cry.

Ten

I couldn't bring myself to harm her. My baby. My only daughter. She wasn't hard to restrain. I swaddled her in the flannel blanket we kept folded at the end of the bed.

It had been months since I'd last swaddled her. She's grown so much since then, since those first few days at the hospital. I wrapped her like a mummy, and with her still twitching inside the casings of the blanket like a pupa, I buried her in the back yard, under the oak tree where I had planned to put up a tire swing for her when she got a little older.

Eleven

Two nights after I buried Alison, the moaning began. Susanna had been such a dedicated mother. I never should've separated them.

When I close my eyes, I picture my wife smiling. There's a halo of morning light surrounding her as she stands by the living room windows. I remember the sunlight playing over her dark hair. God, I miss her. I miss her scent. The sound of her voice. I have horrific dreams of her walking in torment, forever trying to leave, yet trapped in a tangible darkness that rolls over her like a tide that never recedes.

Having nothing else to do but dwell on your thoughts and dreams will drive you to madness. Man was not intended to live this way—isolated and in constant fear.

I hear Alison beneath the old tree, clicking her blackened tongue. Making sucking sounds. Worming through the ground in her cloth casing, always wriggling, always seeking the bottle left for her in the crib. In my head, I hear her crying and afraid and hungry. Her voice scratches inside my skull, trying to get out.

Twelve

This morning I took a shovel, and while the weather was still good, I dug up Alison. Her blanket was soiled from burial, but to my shock, she still moved as though alive. Like a sixteen pound grub worming around inside a chrysalis of filth, she writhed in my arms as I cradled her to my chest and carried her across the yard.

I had to free her, you understand. It was the right thing to do. I couldn't leave her to suffer alone. I took the baby and gave her back to her mother, where she belongs. I whispered, "I love you" in her ear before I dropped her down the well. Then I waited until I heard her strike the water. When it was done, I turned away and went back into the house.

Thirteen

Sitting alone with no one to call, no one to talk to, I've finally decided what I must do next. After all, I'm a family man, married for better or worse.

Susanna and Alison are together now, and soon I will be with them. Earlier today, I took a short rope from the barn, wound it around the bucket pulley for the old well, and made a noose. If you find this notebook, know that I tried to be the best husband I could be. The best father I could be, too. I can't live with my heart so empty. I'm going to place this notebook in the roll-top desk for safekeeping. That way, anyone who finds it will understand what has happened and know where we are. That we are okay.

My only regret is that I didn't stay with Susanna every minute. But they are not the only ones who have suffered. Guilt ravages the mind and body like any other plague. I never should have left them. Not for any reason. I should have been here, at the house, watching over my daughter and protecting my wife. I should've been here to hold Susanna's hand through whatever hell she went through in the end. We took our vows seriously when we married. To love and to cherish. To be there for one another always.

Today I'm renewing those vows—in love, in life, and in death. When I look at Susanna's picture on the mantle, her smile fills me with love even as it breaks my heart. The tears won't stop. Every breath I take fills me with pain and shame. I want so much to hold my wife. To hear her voice. In every prayer I speak, I beg her to forgive me.

Oh honey, I'm so sorry. If I could take your place, I'd do it in a heartbeat. No second thoughts. But I'm going to make it up to both you and Alison. I'll spend the rest of eternity making up for that day I left you. Let my last words be a promise to you. I love you both with all my heart. I'll be joining you soon, and I swear we'll never be apart again.

Preview for Cora Zane's

How to Date an Android

Chapter One
New Georgetown, Carolina Islands
2205

It's Friday, the second week of November, and Caitlyn Quincy braves the biting cold to eat a sandwich by the fountain in Market Square. All around her, the shopping district bustles with midday foot traffic, while the New Georgetown clock tower overlooking it all ticks off the remaining minutes of her lunch hour in distant silence. She sits where she always does, facing the park, which is nothing more than a grassy slope that stretches between the cobbled quad and the narrow jogging track along the murky, Iron River.

Icy wind whips up off the choppy waters of the canal, stirring Caitlyn's long ginger hair and tangling it across her face. She shakes her head to free herself, a gesture that sends the birds hanging around the enormous central fountain into a frenzied flutter of anticipation.

The birds frighten her if they get too close. She's wary of those noisy wings and shell-like beaks. Out of the corner of her eye, she watches them hopping along the ground. They're completely fearless when it comes to people and she admires them for that, but only in the skeptical way an amateur artist might care to admire a rival's painting—best carried out from afar.

With a gloved hand, she brushes away the stray strands of flyaway hair clinging at the side of her mouth before she takes another bite of sandwich. There isn't much in this section of the city to lend convenience to human living anymore, but the hum of persistent traffic and the view of the river are familiarities she isn't yet willing to give up. That much she's inherited from her late father. That, his little shop, and his stubborn unwillingness to follow his neighbors, who all gradually moved away to the human run communities strewn throughout the Mainland and along the Southern Farming Belt.

Her father is gone now, dead for some five years. Nothing holds her here anymore. She could leave the city if she wanted to. One of those secluded, farming communes would surely take her in, but she was born on this island. The Market District has been her neighborhood since she was a little girl. She belongs here just as much as the androids that have turned the area into a chic borough for artificial living.

Caitlyn takes another bite of tomato sandwich and watches the pigeons shuffle closer. They are shameless, the birds. Practiced beggars. She shoos the closest ones away with her boot. They would land on her and eat her lunch if she'd let them.

It isn't easy to do with her gloved fingers, but she pinches off a chunk of bread crust left over from her sandwich and tosses it down, watching the closest birds hop toward it, wings fluttering.

She dreads going back to the shop, but the moon-faced tower clock reads twelve-fifty-two.

Already she's lingered too long, and there is still walking to do.

Crumpling the cloth wrapper in her hand, she licks her lips then brushes the crumbs from the front of her red pea coat, which she wears knotted at the waist with a matching belt. She wishes now she'd brought something to drink, a juice or seltzer water, but a quick glance around for a vending machine to buy something proves fruitless. She's not surprised. Those older style vending machines have been vanishing for some time, like so many other relics from the not so distant past.

Where the old vending machines used to stand, there are now pushcart vendors, recharger spas, and chic cafes. Iron tables sport colorful umbrellas, which hang over red bistro chairs where no one sits. Instead, elegant people wearing the latest in high fashion walk along the promenade, a tree-lined walkway that stretches along the northernmost plaza of businesses. It makes up the greater part of the square, and it's not uncommon to see copycat faces in varying colorations pass by again and again.

There are goddess-like women with abundant marigold curls and radiant, licorice complexions. Ice queens with sultry blue eyes, flawless bone structure, and hair the color of beach sand. Androids covet conformity in all its constructed deviations. Dressed in the height of fashion, they are a rainbow of strutting birds, their slender figures exaggerated by their bold clothes and stylish halo hats. She notices the same asymmetrical wool dress on at least five different women, each garment a varying pop of color—black, red, yellow, teal, then blue.

The men are similarly astounding—statuesque and built. Many have bronze hair today, she notices. It must be a new fad. Various shades of brown have been made in the attempt to copy the trend: chestnut and sienna, all the way to brownish copper.

Everyone is tall, graceful, and perfectly formed, and Caitlyn knows every person she sees belongs to a subset matrix that has been manufactured in limited production runs. She's read articles on how different bio-development companies use aesthetic specialists to choose each model type for production. Their decision is always based on the current interpretation of humankind's ideal appearance, whatever that happens to be.

Caitlyn has a suspicion her lack of physical refinement is yet another reason she draws so many lingering glances. Ripe with all her natural, human imperfections, she's sure the androids must find her greatly flawed.

For the most part, she's used to being stared at and considers it a normal response well within the androids' parameters. Slight framed and short, she is ethnic Irish and unmistakably human. Her heart shaped face isn't the same mask of perfection as the synthetics. Her moss green eyes are too small, and her upper lip is slightly fuller than her lower lip. Although her nose is slender and well formed, it's freckled and unsophisticated in its shape. Someone might consider her cute or interesting looking, but she can't imagine anyone ever describing her as ideal or goddess-like.

A lone human in a city of synthetics, that small truth doesn't bother her as much as it had in the past. Back then, she'd been self-conscious and in her teens, and oh, how she'd wished it possible to emulate the kind of manufactured beauty the androids all share. Only with age has she come to appreciate her uniqueness. In no one else could she hope to find her mother's eyes or her father's dimples.

Let them stare. She's twenty-seven now and in good health. No matter how well she takes care of herself, she won't look like this forever. Besides, she has no reason to be ashamed.

A loud bark makes her jump, and she immediately turns her attention across the quad. The on the grassy slope, a man plays with a beautiful golden retriever. That's a high priced toy—the dog. But what truly stands out is the man himself, his uniqueness. So much so Caitlyn's heart skips a beat. He looks human. His face isn't like any of the others she's seen before—therefore he must be human, right?

She wants to believe, but his features are a little too perfect, rugged in the way of a catalog Adonis with his straight nose and wide kissable mouth. Black hair is her favorite, and his is shiny and short. She can't see the color of his eyes, usually a telltale giveaway, but they crinkle at the corners in a striking way when he smiles, which is what he's doing now—smiling at the dog.

Who wouldn't notice him? Lean and well built, he's at least six feet in height—tall, but not toweringly so. He's dressed for a day in the park. Caitlyn eyes his jeans and the hooded, navy sweatshirt from the university. Does that mean he's educated, not simply programmed? The thought makes her breath catch. After all, he's *her* ideal image of masculine male beauty.

The dog drops a tennis ball at the man's feet. He snaps it up and tosses it across the grassy median. The dog races off to fetch it, and the man cheers, "Thatta boy! Go get it!"

Caitlyn admires the angle of the stranger's square jaw. She imagines the prickly texture of his five o'clock shadow and her fingertips tingle restlessly. It's rude to stare at real people, if that's what he is, but she can't seem to help herself.

The dog returns, ball in mouth, and the man goes down on one knee in the grass. He's full of praise for his large, wiggling pet. There is no mistaking his affection for the animal. He gives its golden coat a brisk rub and a hearty pat to its flanks, and a small smile quirks her lips. They are quite a pair.

As if he somehow senses her watching him, he lifts his head and looks right at her. A jolt of awareness rattles her, and she can't ignore the fluttery feeling that blossoms inside her. Caught in the act, her smile fades. He's not a human after all. Even at a distance, she can see his eyes are resolution blue.

Knowing now what he is, maintaining eye contact is too uncomfortable. It's too intimate and makes her feel on display. With a hollow heart, she averts her eyes and makes an obvious gesture of tucking the sandwich wrapper into her bag. Then she dusts off her gloves. It's a gray day, but she'll miss it once she's back working inside.

She pulls the straps of her tote bag over her shoulder, and out of the corner of her eye, she sees that the handsome android has stopped playing with his dog. He's utterly focused on her. She sighs to herself. *Way to go.* By now, he must surely realize she's human.

In the distance, the tower clock chimes the hour. Face flushed, Caitlyn turns away and walks toward High Street in the direction of her shop, her heart racing against her ribs. Although she knows he's not like her in the human sense, she has to force herself not to glance back to see if he's still watching her.

ABOUT THE AUTHOR

Cora Zane lives in an area of northern Louisiana known as "out in the sticks". She has published a number of stories in multiple genres, including erotic paranormal romance, contemporary erotica, and horror. You can find out more about Cora and her fiction online at **www.corazane.com**.

Also by Cora Zane

What She Doesn't Know

Wave Rider

How to Date an Android

Under A Midnight Moon

Heart Spell

My Zombie Ex-Boyfriend

Heart on Fire

Coming Soon

Twilight's Edge: A Collection of Erotic Fairy Tales

Vampyre Night

Werekind: The Silver Edition

www.grrlxpublishing.com

www.ingramcontent.com/pod-product-compliance
Lightning Source LLC
Chambersburg PA
CBHW070222140626
46555CB00018B/1173